THIS BLOKE
IN THE
Village

*A compact collection of poems & short stories
based around an English village during
2020's Covid-19 pandemic*

By
Tom Bright

This Bloke in the Village

Copyright © 2020 by Tom Bright

All rights reserved. No part of this publication may be reproduced, distributed or transmitted in any form or by any means, including photocopying, recording, or other electronic or mechanical methods, without the prior written permission of the publisher, except in the case of brief quotations embodied in critical reviews and certain other noncommercial uses permitted by copyright law.

*This little book is for anyone
who lost their marbles in 2020...*

That's most of us then.

CONTENTS

This Bloke in the Village 1
Local Lockdown 3
The Dog at Number 12 5
Sod's Law 11
Our Garden 17
The Scarecrow Competition 19
I Really Hope They Open Things Soon 27

THIS BLOKE IN THE VILLAGE

There's this bloke in the village. I don't know his name, what road he lives on or owt, but I tell you what: he bloody stinks. I've clocked him in The Queen's from time to time and there's always this terrible pong following him about. Could turn milk, that man.

Here's a little story. I'm out with our Sandra last week, think it were Wednesday. Despite the rain, we went out on our routine stroll to stretch the legs and see what was occurring. Popped into Barry's to grab a couple of sausage rolls and some eggs then nipped across to the newsagent for ciggies and the telepages.

I'm in there chatting with Linda behind the counter - Sandra's outside observing government guidelines - when in wanders this bloke. I can't see him mind. Don't have eyes in the back of me head! But by god, I recognized that stench.

What with this Corona stuff we're all meant to be social distancing, right? Well, not this cretin. In he comes, reeking to the high heavens, looking like something the cat had dragged in, and he's right up in me space. Can feel the bastard breathing down the back of me neck, he's that close.

Excuse me, I say, *d'ya mind?* Not an effing word back. So I says again, *you deaf or what?*

Now I'll admit it, I've been a bugger in the past and a placid temper isn't exactly something I've been best known for. Linda's trying to get the money out of me, clocking the red mist. I'm at boiling point and my angel's not there to pull me back. I'm all set to turn round and put the nut on this knob head.

Then I think: hold on, he probably lives a life of grime and is a prime bloody candidate to be carrying this thing about.

Now, I don't want to take that home and be the death of the wife, do I. Can you imagine? So I can't even touch this twat for worry of catching something!

I can't believe I'm even telling you this, but I pay Linda, keep me head down and walk out.

Right pain in the arse this virus, isn't it...

LOCAL LOCKDOWN

Across the county border they come in droves

Their cars roar down our quiet roads
Descending upon our well-stocked shops

Emptying the shelves and they cannot stop

Leaving their litter scattered across our peaks

Scaring the life out of our sheep
Drinking pints in our pubs

Meeting their mates for long lost hugs

Bugger off!

THE DOG AT NUMBER 12

What is it they say – a dog is a man's best friend? They'd clearly not met Denzyl, the loud mouth Staffordshire Bull Terrier at 12 Crab Tree Close.

For postman Trevor Collins, life had been shitting on him from a great height. What with the pandemic taking his old man's life and supplying his own daily workload with twenty-too-many Amazon parcels, he really wasn't in the mood on this Groundhog Monday. Lockdown had given a local hero a lonely funeral, and as Trev was one of the nation's 'key workers', time off to grieve was nigh on impossible.

Another no-go was proper social interaction - nothing beyond the occasional chat through a half-opened window to a couple of the elders in the retirement bungalows. He'd found himself looking forward to talking at the Aldi checkout girl before closing time.

Anyway, he's out doing the rounds on this particular miserable morning when most folk are on furlough. Number eight ordering box-upon-box of mail-order dross as per. He thought, *God knows what/they do for a living, but they've got far too much money, that lot.*

At number ten it looked like a birthday. Couple of cards. *Shite party that'd be,* he secretly wished.

Arriving onto number twelve's front garden path, Trevor was well aware of this protective pooch guarding the place. The squeaky gate still hadn't had its WD-40 fix, and he knew the slightest sound was going to set this nutty mut off.

Easy did it. Slowly moly...

Then: *WOOF, WOOF, WOOOOOOF!*

Shhiiiit...

This is where it takes an unexpected turn. The devil-in-disguise-dog, heading straight for him, suddenly stopped in its tracks, stood up on both back legs and started to strut over, as cool as you like.

Trevor was totally nonplussed...

Denzyl the dog, assuming this newly adopted human character, pulled a cigar of all things from behind his left ear, a lighter from behind his right, and blazed it up like a seasoned Mafioso.

"Hey Posty. I gotta bone to pick witchu..."

At this point, with his feet firmly fixed to the ground and his jaw practically touching his toes, Trevor didn't know whether he were coming or going. Trying to talk, he just blurted out stuttered squirms. Suddenly nothing about this situation made any sense whatsoever.

Closer and closer Denzyl was getting. Almost nose-to-nose, he blew a thick ring of smoke straight into Trevor's face. *How was he talking? How was he walking? How was he SO TALL?*

"I seen you, slouched down like the world owes you a big fat one. You really think that kinda attitude is gonna get you outta this rut?"

"W, w.. wha?" The plot thickened. The dog had the accent of an old-school New York taxi driver.

"Listen, don't w, w, w me, OK. I'm just trying to save your sorry ass from the depths of despair...

I get it – you lost someone, you're stressed up to the eyeballs with work, the world's in a mess, everyone's got someone except you, yaddy yaddy yadda. But do you really think that this moping around is gonna get you anywhere? If you do, you're wronger than the world's wrongest man on Wrong Day.

You need to grieve, kid – one-hundred-thousand-percent! And, after that, you need to start taking responsibility for your own life.

I've clocked you begrudgingly judging those parcels in your sack. Envying the big houses in the hood, thinking 'why them, what did they do to deserve this...' Moan, moan. It's booooring..."

Denzyl, now leaning on the fence with his left paw, continued in a calmer, more composed manner.

"You're a good guy, Trevor. Deep down inside, you're a kind man – I can see that. You work yourself to the bone to please others, and boy – I love a good bone. But are you pleasing yourself? Tell me - are you any nearer to getting that holiday let that you've always dreamt of?"

Trevor was without words. He'd been bamboozled into bewilderment. *How on earth did he know about that?*

"Take the time off, get your head together, read some books, relax the mind and start living the life you wanna live. Grab the bull by the horns, 'cos its too short – trust me. I'm pushing sixteen in human

years. That's eighty in dog years! My number's nearly up...

I've had a good innings. I chased a few balls. I bit a few legs. No one needs to worry about me!

Inject some meaning into your existence, and who knows – maybe you'll stop concerning yourself with number eight's excessive orders?"

Then, as if a balloon popped in his brain, he found himself pinned down on the grass with a big, smelly, soft-as-grease Staffy on top of him, licking his lips all over. The post scattered across the lawn, he looked to one side and saw some slippers fast-approaching.

"Denzyl. Denzyl! Oh, my gosh – I am so, so, so sorry about him. I know he gives it the biggun, but he's lovely really. DENZYL, COME HERE!"

Rising to his feet, dusting himself off, trying to figure out exactly what had just happened, Trevor regained a grasp of where he was and looked up at this very pleasant looking lady that he'd never actually spoken to.

"Ohhh, don't be daft. I'm fine, I'm fine, honestly. I know he was only trying to be nice!"

She was talking frantically, trying to pick up the letters in an attempt to make amends for what had just happened. *"I feel so bad. I do hope you're OK?*

The intimidating façade is all for show with him. He really isn't a bad dog. In fact, he's been the best company I could've wished for. I don't know what I'd have done without him..."

"Yes, of course, of course. I'm a postman – we're used to being knocked out by dogs!"

They both chuckled, she handed over the mail at arm's length and Denzyl seemed to be smiling at Trevor.

Conversation continued between these new acquaintances. "*I know we have to remain two-metres apart, but do you, I dunno, fancy a cuppa? I can bring a couple of chairs out here and space them out...*"

And the rest is history.

SOD'S LAW

The village was waking up to a wet Wednesday in early June. Cats and dogs were coming down from the sky, and the gardens were soaking up all they could after a couple of scorching months.

Colin Cobble, who had lived at 53 Druffield Road for all of his up-to-this-point pointless-ish life, lay snuggled up beneath the warmth of his bed sheets.

A gale blew against the single-glazed panes that were fitted when the building went up in the forties, and the rain clung to the glass, blurring the morning view.

He surfaced from his usual left side, stretched and released an over-exaggerated yawn. In the corner of his time-warped room stood a nineteen-sixties television set on stick-like legs. He turned it on and tweaked the tuning to the nearest channel. No Netflix in this household.

Out the bedroom, onto the staircase that he used to bomb down in a cardboard box as a boy, he flicked the kettle on and noticed the postman had been. An envelope lay on mat, simply hand-written *This Weekend*.

He recited to himself in the kitchen, *Cups out, bags in, sugar ready, water up to almost the brim,* then shouted upstairs: *"Want one, Dad?"*

Nowt. Brew en route in any case.

Colin was your typical live and die in the same town type. He'd started out as the local paperboy aged twelve and moved up to the garden centre on his sixteenth birthday. He had occupied the role of Odd Job Boy ever since and was rumoured around the place to be a bit of an unknown, due to his habit of keeping himself to himself.

He stared outside whilst stirring the teabags and thanked his stars it was his day off. That downpour would've seen him turned into a drowned rat, and since they'd reopened horticultural sites, it'd been hell for him and his walkie-talkie.

Equipped with two cups of Yorkshire's finest, he trotted back upstairs to deliver his Dad's wake-up call. Tapping on the door, he eased it ajar and popped the steaming mug on the far side of the room. What with him now working during the pandemic, he was being extremely cautious when it came to keeping his distance from his elderly old man.

Softly he spoke, *"Morning Dad. Sleep alright?"* Not a peep.

Colin got back into his own bed and proceeded to watch whatever was on. A newsreader was reporting yet another crime across the pond, and he was made more certain that the planet was becoming scarier by the day. He felt safe where he was.

A few swigs in, basking in the bliss of a locked down day off (albeit it a rainy one), he remembered the mail downstairs, fetched it off the floor by the front door and brought it back up to bed. He ran his thumb along the inside of the envelope and brought out a very small note.

DON'T FORGET UPPER TITCHWORTH SCARECROW COMPETITION THIS SATURDAY!

Well, it'd be no replacement for the cancelled Carnival but might be nice for some folk, he thought. No intention of entering himself though.

Slurping away, half paying attention to the world's continuing chaos on the small screen, he heard an almighty fart echo down the hall, announcing that his Dad had awoken to see another day. *"Thanks for the tea, son!"*

Ever since Colin's Mam passed away, him and his old Dad Roger Cobble had really tightened their relationship. They went on fishing trips together and played in the darts team at The Queen's. This Covid-19 had stripped them of these simple bonding pleasures and forced them both into living fairly separately under the same roof.

Colin's work had him sweating buckets as soon as he started his shift, and he was well aware he probably stunk. They'd not even provided him with many sets of uniform, so sometimes he'd have to go in wearing the mucky clobber from the day before. It was time to do some washing.

He took his dirty laundry bag down to the kitchen and started to load the machine. Every stitch he had needed to go through – and as for the socks, they were close to crawling!

His Dad had found his way out of bed and spoke from the second-to-top step on the stairwell. *"Sleep alright, son? Bloody sod's law this weather, eh…"*

"Alright Dad. Yeah, not bad ta. Need anything going in this wash?"

"I don't need any washing doing just yet – but how's about you nip round to the newsagent and grab me today's paper?"

It was still peeing down, and he didn't have owt clean to wear – but he couldn't refuse his old man's request. He took a pair of muddy jeans and a jumper out from the machine he'd just placed them, quickly whipped them on and took a quid from the coin pot. *"Go on then"* he said, jokingly acting out his arm was held up against his back.

Outside, the rain remained. He passed the village hall, the pharmacy, went down the disused railway track and over Barley Bridge. They were forming an orderly queue outside the butcher's again.

He crossed the main road and onto the newsagent. *"You in the queue there, duck?"* he asked a woman, who seemed to be waiting for someone inside to come out. She gave him the nod to go in, and he was greeted by Linda's reliable stern face behind the counter. There was just one chap in front of him grabbing a pack of Marlboro Red and a magazine.

He picked up the paper and waited his turn in line. His mind trailed off for a moment and the guy in front seemed to say something about him before he left, but he wasn't sure.

"Ayup Linda. Just this for today please..."

Linda was a good egg at heart, but she wore a face like a smacked arse and wasn't afraid to call a spade a spade. She seemed to be keeping something back on this particular occasion.

"What d'ya know, owt or nowt?" Colin tried to fill the silence by coaxing something out of her…

She looked him square on with her brows clenched and came out with, *"Well, if you must know, you smell bloody awful!"*

Walking home with his head down to hide his embarrassed beetroot face, paper shoved up his dirty jumper as to keep it dry, the clouds above continued to cry. He wished the over-seventies didn't have to self-isolate for much longer so he didn't have to do all the shopping, and he really hoped the sun would shine, so he could wash and dry his clothes in time for tomorrow's shift.

Sod's law!

OUR GARDEN

There's a blackbird that visits our garden
He sings at the top of his voice
Charming the crows
Serenading the gnomes
To listen, they don't have a choice

Little Robin flies in for a bath
Then dries himself off on the grass
Showing all his red breast
He leaves the ladies impressed
Before attempting to make a cheeky pass

What about that sneaky greenfinch
He'll take a mile if you give him an inch
Swoops down from the trees
Snatches the sunflower seeds
Leaving no trace of a footprint

The most raucous might be the wren
Thinking she's the garden's own big ben
Loudly she chirps
Regular like clockwork
She even drowns out the hens

Sometimes we see that beautiful jay
The most colourful in the community
Residing in the conifers
Hiding from local photographers
She longs for a life of privacy

In the corner stands the old lady
She's soft, albeit made of stone
Doesn't make a peep
Never gets a wink of sleep
I hope she doesn't feel too alone

It's sad that it took us to pause
To really notice the noise
Without the traffic's boom
We paid attention to the bloom
And embraced our garden's simple joys

THE SCARECROW COMPETITION

Saturday 6th June dawned. It marked the first ever Scarecrow Competition in Upper Titchworth, and on Bramble Lane you could cut the tension with a knife.

Over the years, a bitter feud had developed between Beryl Burley at number seven and Mary Stewart at number nine. Both wives rather house-proud, there was an ongoing conflict between them: who had the nicest car, who showcased the best-looking Christmas decorations, who had the most talented children, and so on.

It's not nice when a neighbour becomes your worst nightmare and Mary Stewart's recent antics had become a major thorn in Beryl Burley's side.

She'd been throwing tea parties in her back garden during quarantine, and Beryl was close to dobbing her in to the bobbies.

They'd spotted each other down at the local garden centre during the week. Their eyes met at the till, and Mary cast Beryl one of those sarcastic smiles of hers. Beryl scowled back and the scene was set for a fiery day.

"She makes my blood boil", Beryl would complain through gritted teeth to her husband Pete. *"I mean she is such a bitch. I HAVE to win this competition!"*

The stakes were high. Conquer this, and the bragging rights would be far too much for the loser to contend with. They'd spent all week preparing their entries behind closed doors to unleash them upon each other on judgement day.

Well, that morning had arrived, and as Phil Stewart was in the kitchen at number nine eating crumpets, reading the paper, trying to keep out the way of his wife Mary, she was causing all kinds of chaos, tear-arsing around the house trying to put the finishing touches on her Bee Gee-inspired production. *"ARE YOU GOING TO GIVE ME A HAND WITH THIS THING OR WHAT?"* It sounded like Diablo itself had summoned the demand.

Reluctantly closing the pages with his buttery fingers, he made his way to the living room whilst licking them off. There she was, curlers in, dressing gown on, looking like Worzel Gummidge gone wrong. She happened to see him roll his eyes in the mirror. *"TAKE THIS!"*

She sent a shoe flying straight for his head. *"CALM DOWN WOMAN"*, he cried.

The kids had learned a couple of days previous to avoid their Mother pre-competition, and Phil had found himself directly in the line of fire. She smacked him full-blown in the bollocks. He bent over and it was then that she slapped the back of his baldhead. *"You do as I say, OK!"*

Without further ado, he was tending to her on hand and foot. He pulled the flares up on its rake spine, put its sparkly jacket on and had been forced to donate his expensive sunglasses. The wig went on as Mary Stewart sat back in awe of her very own Sir Barry Gibb. *"If this doesn't win it, my name is Mickey Mouse…"*

Next door at number seven, it was a similar scenario. Beryl Burley had already booted her husband Pete in the shin. He had become a shadow of his former self, and quivered in his slippers as he held her scarecrow up whilst she placed its high-heels on. She had attempted to reincarnate Tina Turner.

Pete's dedication to the cause had actually outdone Phil Stewart's. Beryl Burley had forced her husband into shaving his head. He said no. She walloped him. He said yes. Beryl then taped his hair to the tips of her existing wig, and Tina had a long mane to match her nineties look.

Anyway, he's there bald as a coot, shaking like a shitting dog. She'd stripped him of his hair and not even given him time for breakfast. Tina Turner stood tall in her party shoes, ready to rock.

There were clear instructions set out that all entries had to be placed on the front gardens by midday. Former Post Office proprietor Albert Monk was to be the judge. It was three minutes to. Screams from inside the abodes could be heard outside on the street. Emerging at precisely the same time, both parties pretended all was cool and calm. The husbands carried out the wives' prized possessions, placing them in position whilst acknowledging each other's battle wounds. They prepared for the moderator to pass by.

"What the hell is that supposed to be?"

"... the state of it!"

The counterparts couldn't help criticise each other's creations.

It was ten past twelve, and Albert had arrived on their lane with his clipboard, scoring them as he went on by. Beryl at number seven showered him with well wishes and shouted, *"do send your good lady Marg my love!"*

Working his way to number nine, Mary Stewart ran inside to fetch the trick she had concealed up her sleeve. She'd baked the judge a carrot cake! *"Wait there Albert!"* She quickly grabbed the tin from inside the porch, ran back outside and placed it on the table at the top of the lawn, next to the fence.

"How kind of you Mary, thank you!" Albert said. *"It's my pleasure"*, she replied, smiling slyly like a silent assassin who'd just eliminated her competitor. She held the expression and turned her head in the direction of number seven to see Beryl absolutely beside herself. If looks could kill!

The winner was to be announced in The Upper Titchworth Gazette the following morning. A sleepless night ensued for Beryl and Mary. They kept their husbands up all night with incessant nervous ramblings.

Eight AM on Sunday, and the usual grumpy postman seemed to have a spring in his step. He skipped between addresses, posting the paper through the desperate letterboxes. The wives scrambled to their respective doors. Mary Stewart even caught her paper before it'd hit the carpet.

From butterflies in the stomach to a stark sickness, it was official…

The winner of our very first Upper Titchworth Scarecrow Competition is… Doris Delaney at 66 Lavender Row!

"THAT OLD HAG!"

"ARRRGGGGHHHHHHHH!"

The rooftops trembled for the expletives. It was F-word this, C-bomb that. The kids had never heard such filth.

As if twinned by an unexplainable spiritual connection, both wives suddenly fell silent and stepped outside in their nighties armed with fire-lighting tools. Not a word spoken in an almost possessed-like state, they set off with satanic strides to pay little old Irish Doris a visit. It was like a rare moon was calling them

Meanwhile at number sixty-six Lavender Row, sweet old Missus Delaney was made up. She was in her armchair on the phone to her daughter. Her husband Seamus would've been delighted. *"God rest his soul"*, she said, wiping the tears from behind her glasses.

Then her false teeth nearly fell out, as she looked outside to see two silhouettes set against the morning sun. In a flash, the champion scarecrow was up in flames. It was like something from The Wicker Man, with the two ladies in their nighties looking on at the crime they had just committed.

"Mum.. Mum..?"

But the phone line went dead.

Rumour is Beryl and Mary get on alright these days. Not sure what happened to Doris though.

I REALLY HOPE THEY OPEN THINGS SOON

Hash-tagging bandwagons from slave-made phones
Posted from the comfort of safe suburban homes

People on furlough with far too much time
In a woke competition blurring the lines

The cringe-worthy, white middle-class
Ranting it's wrong to have any kind of laugh

Without understanding the nature of a joke
Just wanting to paint himself as a virtuous bloke

Last week he tweeted that all in the park
Were a bunch of Grandma-murderers at heart

But now he's squashed up in a tin of sardines

Down Trafalgar Square causing a scene

With new Nike trainers on stitched by nine-year-old hands
From the same factory as his old knackered Vans

It's a good job that the weather turned out good
Because he didn't fancy parading them out in mud

'Clapping for Carers' – mate, it's my Mum who's a nurse
And all she wanted was a few more quid in her purse

To be paid properly for what she's done for forty-six years
Not you standing on your doorsteps judging your neighbouring peers

Did we all wash our hands of actual common sense?
When did we become so extreme both sides of the fence?

I really hope they open things soon
Or the internet will burst like a bullshit balloon

Printed in Great Britain
by Amazon